The
MAGNIFICENT
MAKERS

Race Through Space

Go on more
a-MAZE-ing adventures with

The
MAGNIFICENT
MAKERS

How to Test a Friendship

Brain Trouble

Riding Sound Waves

The Great Germ Hunt

Race Through Space

The MAGNIFICENT MAKERS

5

Race Through Space

by Theanne Griffith
illustrated by Reggie Brown

A STEPPING STONE BOOK™
Random House 🏠 New York

Visit us on the Web!
rhcbooks.com

Educators and librarians, for a variety of teaching tools, visit us at
RHTeachersLibrarians.com

Library of Congress Cataloging-in-Publication Data
Names: Griffith, Theanne, author. | Brown, Reggie, illustrator.
Title: Race through space / by Theanne Griffith; illustrated by Reggie Brown.
Description: First edition. | New York: Random House Children's Books, 2022. |
Series: The magnificent makers; 5 | Summary: Pablo loves everything outer space, but as he, Violet, and Deepak go through the levels of the Maker Maze to learn about space, he keeps making mistakes, and his friends keep correcting him, so he begins to wonder whether he will ever know enough to become an astronaut.
Identifiers: LCCN 2021004763 (print) | LCCN 2021004764 (ebook) |
ISBN 978-0-593-37963-9 (paperback) | ISBN 978-0-593-37964-6 (library binding) |
ISBN 978-0-593-37965-3 (ebook)
Subjects: LCSH: Makerspaces—Juvenile fiction. | Space sciences—Juvenile fiction. |
Friendship—Juvenile fiction. | Outer space—Juvenile fiction. |
Solar system—Juvenile fiction. | CYAC: Makerspaces—Fiction. | Space sciences—
Fiction. | Friendship—Fiction. | Outer space—Fiction. | Solar system—Fiction.
Classification: LCC PZ7.1.G7527 Rac 2022 (print) | LCC PZ7.1.G7527 (ebook) |
DDC 813.6 [Fic]—dc23

Printed in the United States of America
10 9 8 7 6 5 4 3 2

First Edition

This book has been officially leveled by using
the F&P Text Level Gradient™ Leveling System.

For Lila corazón, my future astronaut
—T.G.

To Kaia, Bella, and Indigo,
I wish for you all the happiness
this world has to offer
—R.B.

Sluuuuuuuuuuuuuurp!

Pablo sucked an imaginary string of pasta through his lips.

"No way!" said Violet with squinted eyes. She tucked a few stray kinks of hair behind her ears and crossed her arms. "That's impossible."

"I promise! That's what happens if you get too close to a black hole," replied Pablo. "I read all about it. You get stretched like a *looooooooooong* piece of spaghetti."

"Well . . . I'm glad there aren't any black

holes close to Earth," said Violet. "I can't become a scientist if I get turned into a noodle first."

The two best friends giggled. They sat cross-legged in the center of the Newburg Meadow with tall grass and scattered flowers fluttering in the wind around them. The field was dotted with Newburg Elementary students and their families. This month's field trip was outdoors, and everyone was waiting for the sun to go down. Tonight, they were going to watch one of the largest meteor showers ever recorded in New-burg history!

"Did you know a meteor shower happens when lots of tiny bits of space rock

come close
to Earth and
burn up?"
asked Pablo
in one long
breath. "Some-
times people call
them shooting stars.
But they're not even stars!" Pablo could
hardly contain his excitement.

"Yes, you told me yesterday. And the
day before that." Violet laughed.

Pablo and Violet had been best friends
since Pablo moved from Puerto Rico to
Newburg in first grade. They'd play soccer
together in the park after school or share
a delicious pickle on their walk home.
But this week, Pablo had spent all his free
time in the library reading about meteors
and other space objects. Both Pablo and

Violet loved learning about science. But space was Pablo's favorite. And he wanted to make sure he remembered *everything* for tonight's field trip.

Pablo's mom called from across the meadow. "It's almost time!" She held her watch in the air and tapped it. "Only fifteen more minutes until sunset."

Violet's dad was standing next to Pablo's mom. He gave Pablo and Violet two thumbs-up.

Pablo tilted his head back and looked at the deep-purple-and-pink sky. One day he was going to watch a meteor shower from the window of his very own space-ship. That had been his dream ever since he could remember, even though some of his cousins would tease him about it. They said he was too forgetful to become an astronaut. But today he was prepared.

"Hi!" said a voice suddenly.

Pablo and Violet looked over their shoulders. It was their friend Deepak!

"Hey!" said Pablo. He eyed a pair of binoculars hanging around Deepak's neck. "Where did you get those?"

"They belong to my mom. She let me borrow them for the meteor shower. They're kind of heavy, though." Deepak removed the binoculars and set them in the grass. Then he plopped down next to Pablo. "This is going to be so awesome!" Deepak rubbed the palms of his hands together.

"It won't actually *rain* meteors tonight,

right?" Violet asked. She bit her lip and looked up at the darkening sky.

"Nah!" replied Deepak. "Most meteors are too small. They just burn up."

"That's true. But did you know *thousands* of meteors still hit Earth every year?" added Pablo. "I wouldn't be surprised if tonight— Oh no! Look out!"

Violet yelped and covered her face with her hands. Nothing happened. She peeked through the cracks in her fingers and saw Pablo and Deepak smiling.

"Not funny, Pablo!" she said. Then she smiled, too.

2

"**G**lad to see you all having fun," said Mr. Eng. The trio looked up. Their teacher stood above them with a smile on his face and a pencil behind his ear. He was holding a stack of black papers.

"I wish the sun would hurry up and set," said Pablo.

Mr. Eng laughed. "Don't worry. Just a few more moments and we should be able to see the meteor shower."

"What are those, Mr. Eng?" Violet pointed to the papers he was holding.

"These are worksheets about the different objects that exist in our solar system," he replied.

"Like planets!" said Deepak.

"And comets!" added Pablo.

"Exactly," replied Mr. Eng.

"But we won't be able to read those in the dark!" said Violet.

Mr. Eng smiled again and took the stack of papers from under his arm. Green letters glimmered on each sheet.

"Whoa!" said Pablo, Violet, and Deepak.

"I wish all my homework glowed in the dark!" said Pablo, holding the paper up close to his face.

"I'm going to hand the rest of them out to the other students and families." Mr. Eng turned and walked toward a group of parents.

Pablo, Violet, and Deepak read aloud together:

A Space Case: Name That Object

Our solar system is made up of the sun and everything that travels around it. But what exactly is in our solar system?

The **sun** is in the center. It's the biggest object you'll find!

Planets are the next largest object in our solar system. They usually have at least one moon.

Asteroids are small chunks of metal and rock.

A **comet** is a chunk of dust and ice. There are billions of comets in our solar system.

A **meteoroid** is a small piece of comet or asteroid. We call it a meteor when it gets close enough to Earth to burn up. If a meteor lands on Earth, it's called a meteorite.

Violet bit her lip. "Dust and ice . . ." She re-read the sentence. "That sounds like a dirty snowball."

Pablo and Deepak laughed.

"I didn't know meteors came from asteroids," said Pablo.

"Really?" asked Deepak. He tugged his ear. "I knew that."

Pablo scratched his cheek. "Well, I mean . . . ," he began. His face turned a little pink. He had been reading about meteors all week. *How did I forget that?* he wondered.

Out of nowhere, a gust of wind blew through the meadow. The trio gripped their worksheets. As the wind settled, they could see a stray black sheet of paper flipping through the air. It landed in the grass.

"I better go get that," said Pablo, standing up. He hurried over toward the piece of paper. But it wasn't a worksheet.

Pablo held the black paper with glowing green words. "It's a riddle!"

Violet and Deepak ran over.

"Does this mean we get to go *back* to the Maker Maze?" Deepak said, staring at the shimmering sheet.

"Oh yeah," said Violet with a wide smile. The light from the riddle made her kinky hair glow like a crown in the dark.

The Maker Maze was a magical laboratory that Pablo, Violet, and Deepak discovered earlier in the school year. It had everything from robots and lasers to microscopes and zero gravity chambers. And to get there, they needed to solve a riddle like this one. The trio wiggled with excitement as they read carefully:

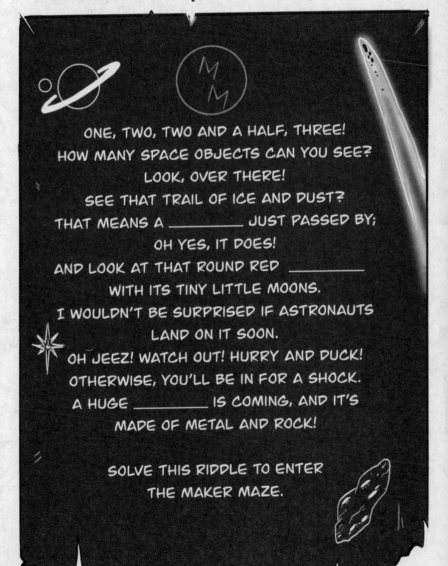

ONE, TWO, TWO AND A HALF, THREE!
HOW MANY SPACE OBJECTS CAN YOU SEE?
LOOK, OVER THERE!
SEE THAT TRAIL OF ICE AND DUST?
THAT MEANS A _____ JUST PASSED BY;
OH YES, IT DOES!
AND LOOK AT THAT ROUND RED _____
WITH ITS TINY LITTLE MOONS.
I WOULDN'T BE SURPRISED IF ASTRONAUTS
LAND ON IT SOON.
OH JEEZ! WATCH OUT! HURRY AND DUCK!
OTHERWISE, YOU'LL BE IN FOR A SHOCK.
A HUGE _____ IS COMING, AND IT'S
MADE OF METAL AND ROCK!

SOLVE THIS RIDDLE TO ENTER
THE MAKER MAZE.

"The first one has to be *comet*," said Violet.

"And the next one is definitely *planet*. It's probably Mars!" added Deepak.

"Which means the last one is *meteoroid*!" shouted Pablo.

Pablo, Deepak, and Violet waited. Nothing happened.

"Maybe it's *asteroid*? Since it's massive?" Violet suggested.

Without warning, the ground began to shake. The grass and flowers vibrated. It felt like the earth was dancing below their feet. Pablo, Violet, and Deepak held on to one another to keep from falling.

BOOM! SNAP! WHIZ! ZAP!

The ground became still. The grass and flowers didn't budge. The three friends slowly wandered around the silent meadow. Each time they opened the portal to the Maker Maze, everyone and everything else froze in place!

"Whoa . . . ," Violet said. "Look at that!" She pointed up. A bat was upside down and frozen midflight! Its mouth was open.

"Must have been chasing after a bug!" said Pablo.

"Oh no!" Deepak shouted.

"What's wrong?" asked Violet.

"My mom's binoculars! I lost them!" Deepak replied.

"Didn't you set them down—" Violet began.

"Over there!" Pablo exclaimed.

They ran over to the pair of binoculars. They were glowing in a circle of purple light. Deepak knelt to pick them up. He felt a tickle on his fingertips as they passed through the light.

BIZZAP!

He giggled as he pulled his hand back.

"I'm sure they'll be fine here," said Violet. She looked around at all the frozen faces. Then she reached one hand down to Deepak and the other to Pablo. "Ready?"

The trio leaned in close to the beaming binoculars.

"Here we go!" Pablo called into the

evening sky. One by one, they were squeezed through the portal.

BIZZAP!

They landed feetfirst on the floor of the Maker Maze. The room was huge and filled with all kinds of fun science equipment. The Makers wandered along the lab tables that held odd plants and flasks of mysterious, bubbling liquids.

"It's even cooler than I remember," said Deepak.

"I think it gets cooler each time we come back," said Violet.

The trio passed by large jars with buzzing bugs and a line of zero gravity chambers that held floating crystals. Next to the never-ending hallway were two robots sitting at a giant microscope. They were taking turns looking through the lens. Across the room, a screen showed that everyone was still frozen in the Newburg Meadow.

"Well, howdy, Makers!" a voice boomed from behind. Pablo, Violet, and Deepak turned and smiled at the tall woman with wild rainbow hair.

"It's *magnificent* to see you again!" Dr. Crisp continued, clapping her hands. "Hey, stranger! Glad you're back," she said to Deepak.

"Me too! I've missed this place," he replied.

"Dr. Crisp! Dr. Crisp!" Pablo shouted as he jumped up and down. "We have to learn about space on this challenge. We were just about to watch a meteor shower before we got your riddle!"

Dr. Crisp smiled and pulled a large umbrella out of the front pocket of her lab coat. She opened it and said, "I'm always prepared for bad weather!"

The Makers laughed.

"It's not *that* kind of shower, Dr. Crisp," said Pablo.

"Yeah," added Deepak. "It's more like fireworks!"

Dr. Crisp winked. "Just

teasing!" She set the umbrella on the floor. "Well, let's get this show on the road!" She went to grab the Maker Manual off a lab table. But it wasn't there.

"Uh-oh." Dr. Crisp removed a pencil from behind her ear and rubbed her chin with the eraser. She snapped her head in one direction, then in the other. She darted up and down along each lab table. Suddenly, she dropped to her hands and knees and squinted at the floor. Finally, she stood up and shrugged.

"What are we going to do?" asked Pablo, scratching his cheek. He really didn't want anything to go wrong today.

"Wait a minute!" said Dr. Crisp. She reached up and dug around in her hair with both hands. She pulled and tugged a bit before removing a glittering lab notebook.

"Well, flip my flask! Forgot that I stuck it up there while I was cleaning. Now, did someone say *space*?" asked Dr. Crisp. She held the golden book in the palms of her hands. It snapped open quickly to a picture of a large question mark.

"Yes!" Pablo, Violet, and Deepak cheered.

The pages of the book began turning quickly. A gust of wind blew through the Maze just like in the Newburg Meadow.

The wind stopped as the pages slowed.
They finally landed on one that read:

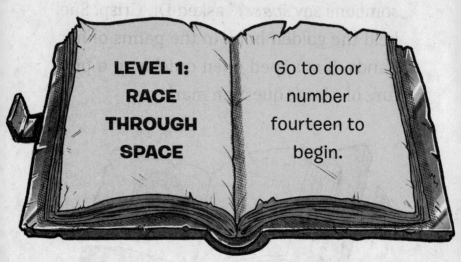

**LEVEL 1:
RACE
THROUGH
SPACE**

Go to door
number
fourteen to
begin.

Pablo felt a warm feeling rise in his
chest. He had never been so excited in his
life. "This is going to be *epic*!"

4

"**M**agnificent Maker Watches ready?" shouted Dr. Crisp. She stood in front of the door with her hand on the knob.

"Yes!" replied the Makers, each holding an arm in the air. These special watches appeared on their wrists when they were about to start the challenge. They used them for all kinds of things in the Maker Maze, like shooting lasers, recording their answers, scanning holograms—and most importantly, keeping track of time.

"Good!" said Dr. Crisp. "We'll be traveling pretty far!"

The Makers needed to finish the challenge in less than one hundred twenty Maker Minutes if they wanted to return to the Maze for more fun. Dr. Crisp slowly opened the door, and the Makers' watches vibrated and glowed.

As Pablo, Violet, and Deepak walked through door number fourteen, their mouths dropped open. Rotating slowly in the middle of the wide room was a model solar system! In the center shone a bright yellow sun. Around it circled the eight different planets. And in between the orange glow of Mars and the stormy surface of Jupiter, tons of different-sized rocks floated like confetti.

Pablo pointed. "That must be the asteroid belt!" He definitely remembered reading about that. "It's the place in our solar system where most of the asteroids are found."

Violet reached out to run her fingertips

through the edge of the model solar system.

BIZZAP!

"Okay, Makers. Listen up! For this level, we're going to get up close and personal with different space objects. But first, we'll need some special equipment!" Dr. Crisp pressed a button on the side of her watch and shouted, "Maker Maze, activate space suits!"

The room immediately went dark, and the floor began to vibrate. Suddenly, a blast of purple light shot out of the model sun and blinded the Makers.

BOOM! SNAP! WHIZ! ZAP!

After a few seconds, they were able to open their eyes again. The model solar system was gone. Pablo slowly lifted his arms to examine them. He patted his chest with his hands. Then he touched the helmet now covering his face.

"This is . . . ," Pablo began. But he couldn't find the word to finish his sentence.

"AMAZING!" Violet yelled as she jumped in the air.

The Makers were now wearing purple space suits! A black *M* was drawn on each of their chests. Clear helmets covered their faces. Dr. Crisp was in a space suit, too! Hers was black with a bright purple *M* on her chest. They all had silver space gloves.

"I can't believe it," said Deepak. "I'm a *real* astronaut!"

"You bet, space cadet!" said Dr. Crisp. "Okay, Makers. We need one last piece of equipment before we start." Dr. Crisp opened her backpack and began to pull out a long rope. She kept pulling . . . and pulling . . . and pulling. With one final tug, she said, "There! Now let's hook ourselves up."

"What is this for?" asked Violet. She looked closely at the four metal clasps attached to the rope.

"It looks like a leash," said Deepak.

"I know what it is!" said Pablo proudly. "It's a space tether!"

"What a *galactic* guess!" said Dr. Crisp. She gave Pablo a high five. "We're going to attach ourselves to this rope so that we all stay together. Wouldn't want anyone to get lost in space!" Dr. Crisp found the end of the very long rope. She tied it to a hook on the floor. Then she yelled into her watch, "Maker Maze, open *wormhole*!"

The ceiling slowly slid open. The Makers could only see blackness. Suddenly, a purple beam of light shot down from above.

"Cool!" said Violet.

"What is a wormhole?" asked Pablo. He started to walk in a circle around the glowing beam of light. "Is it like a portal?"

"No, a portal is more like a door,"

Deepak explained. "A wormhole is like a . . ." He thought for a moment. "A bridge! It connects places in space that are far apart."

"Well, shine my stars!" said Dr. Crisp. "You sure know your space stuff!"

Deepak smiled proudly. But Pablo felt a little bummed. Why didn't *he* know what a wormhole was? Didn't he read enough books at the library?

Dr. Crisp went around and hooked

each Maker's suit to the rope. "Okay, Makers. No time to waste! Who's ready to race through space?" asked Dr. Crisp with a clap of her space gloves.

"We are!" the trio replied.

"Ready, set, BLAST OFF!"

Everyone jumped into the beam of light.

BIZZAP!

5

Swizzzzzzzz!

Pablo, Violet, Deepak, and Dr. Crisp blasted through the wormhole. It felt like they were shooting down an extremely fast and tingly slide. They were moving so fast, it was hard to see anything but streaks of stars around them.

The Makers shouted with delight. It felt like Pablo's dream of becoming an astronaut was finally coming true.

BIZZAP!

They popped out the other end and floated gently through the air.

"Welcome to Magnifica! The Maker Maze's own private galaxy," said Dr. Crisp into her watch.

Deepak was mouthing something, but no one could hear him. Dr. Crisp pointed to his wrist. He pressed a button on his Magnificent Maker Watch and said, "I don't think I've ever seen anything more beautiful in my life!"

The darkness of Magnifica was dotted with the flickering lights of stars. Hazy streaks of pink, green, yellow, and blue swirled in the distance. Violet stretched out her hands and legs and did a slow cartwheel. Pablo leaned back and put his hands behind his head. He took a deep breath and smiled.

"Listen up, Makers!" Dr. Crisp's voice sounded through everyone's helmets. "We are on a mission! A *magnificent* mission! Soon different space objects will blast past us. It's up to you to decide what each object is. You will all need to agree and record your answers using your watches."

"Just how close will we get to these objects?" Violet asked with raised eyebrows. "I don't want to get run over by a planet."

Pablo and Deepak giggled.

"You are always safe in the Maker Maze!" replied Dr. Crisp. "And in Magnifica." She held her three middle fingers down in the shape of an *M*. "Maker's honor!"

Just then, something big and bright came into view. It was moving toward them. And fast!

"Here we go, Makers!" said Dr. Crisp.

Pablo, Violet, and Deepak were ready. The giant space object got closer and closer until it finally passed far to the right. Not only was it huge, but it left a glittery trail behind.

"Whoa, did you see that?" said Deepak.

"How could we miss it? It nearly hit us!" Violet replied.

"Oh, come on! It wasn't that close." Pablo laughed.

Then their watches vibrated. Pablo looked down at his. A flashing arrow appeared. He swiped once. It read *asteroid*. He smiled.

"Hey! I think I know what that was!" Pablo shouted to his friends. "It was an asteroid!" He held up his watch proudly.

Violet bit her lip and shook her head.

"I don't think so, Pablo. It had a tail."

"Yeah, I'm pretty sure it was a comet," added Deepak. "They leave trails like that."

Pablo felt some of his excitement fade. His chest lowered inside his suit. "Oh yeah," he mumbled. Pablo swiped three more times on his watch until the word *comet* appeared. The trio selected it together.

(((((((*RING, DING, DONG!*)))))))

The Maker Maze jingle echoed throughout Magnifica.

"Flamin' jet fuel! Nice work!" cheered Dr. Crisp.

The Makers gave one another high fives. But Pablo was still disappointed in himself. Were his cousins right? Was he too forgetful to be an astronaut?

Suddenly, another space object started hurtling toward them.

"It's huge!" said Violet.

"Is that . . . Mars?" asked Deepak.

"I think so. It's orange," Pablo replied. "And look! It has two moons circling it."

Violet agreed. "Let's try that answer!"

They each selected *planet* on their watches.

RING, DING, DONG!

"Nice work spotting those moons, Pablo!" said Dr. Crisp.

"Thanks," he replied. *At least I got this one right,* he thought.

Next, a giant rock shot past on the right. A few moments later, several smaller rocks flew by on the left.

"I think the first one was an asteroid," said Violet into her watch.

"Yep, and those little ones were meteoroids!" added Deepak.

RING, DING, DONG!

"Roaring rockets!" cheered Dr. Crisp. "Excellent work!"

The Makers came together in a circle to give one another high fives.

Pablo was happy and frustrated at the same time. He wanted to stop making mistakes. He needed to show Violet and Deepak that he knew all about space. He checked his watch, which read eighty-five minutes. "We should head back," he said to the rest of the group.

Dr. Crisp held her hand up to her forehead in a salute. "On it, captain!" She shouted into her watch, "Maker Maze, open wormhole!"

Pablo, Violet, and Deepak felt a tug on their suits. The rope they were attached to was slowly being pulled backward. Then out of nowhere . . .

SWIZZZZZZZZZ!

BIZZAP!

Pablo, Violet, Deepak, and Dr. Crisp were back in room fourteen of the Maker Maze. Their space suits and helmets had disappeared. The space tether lay on the floor.

Dr. Crisp shook out her rainbow hair and found her backpack. She opened it and pulled out the glittery Maker Manual.

"Okay, Makers! Let's find out what's next," she said as the book snapped open.

The pages turned quickly. They opened to one that read:

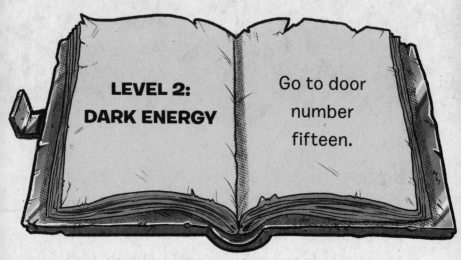

LEVEL 2: DARK ENERGY

Go to door number fifteen.

Dr. Crisp closed the book and tossed it into her backpack. She grabbed the pencil from behind her ear and pointed at the wall opposite the door. "This way!" she hollered over her shoulder.

"Careful, Dr. Crisp!" Deepak shouted across the room.

But just before Dr. Crisp walked

headfirst into the wall, a hidden door slid open. She turned to face the Makers and winked. "What are you waiting for?"

Pablo, Violet, and Deepak hurried through the secret entrance just as the door began to close.

Room number fifteen was empty except for four long poles sticking out of the floor. Each had a hook attached to the middle. Together, the poles formed a large square.

"We just learned about *some* of the different objects you find in space. But there is one space object that we haven't discussed yet," explained Dr. Crisp.

The Makers looked at Dr. Crisp with wide and eager eyes.

"Black holes!" she finally said.

"Yes!" Pablo and Deepak said.

"We're not going to turn into spaghetti,

right?" asked Violet, closing her eyes and biting her lip.

Dr. Crisp laughed. "Don't worry! No *real* black holes in room fifteen. We keep those nice and far away in room three thousand!"

Violet opened her eyes and gulped.

Dr. Crisp continued. "Today, you're going to figure out how black holes work." She got the Maker Manual out of her backpack. It flew open to a page with a list of instructions. Pablo, Violet, and Deepak looked them over. Dr. Crisp reached again into her backpack and started pulling out supplies. She removed a giant black bedsheet, a large black ball, and two smaller purple marbles. Dr. Crisp folded her hands behind her back and started circling the sheet.

"This sheet represents a force that scientists still don't fully understand." Dr. Crisp suddenly leaped in the air and clicked her heels. The room went black. When she landed on the ground, her face was lit up by a flashlight that she held beneath her chin. With a smile, she said, "Scientists call it *dark energy*. And everything in our universe is connected by it."

She turned off the flashlight and clicked her heels again. The light returned.

"Whoa, that sounds creepy," said Violet, blinking. A shiver slid down her spine.

"You can think of dark energy as a fabric. *Space fabric!* That's why we use a sheet to model it," Dr. Crisp continued. "To complete this level, you'll need to figure out how black holes work. But first, you need to make the model," she said, pointing to the instructions.

Pablo rubbed his hands together. His

chest began to rise again with the excitement that had faded during level one. "Let's do this!" he said.

Then Dr. Crisp hollered, "Ready, set, MODEL!"

The trio huddled together.

"I think all we have to do is attach this sheet to the hooks," said Pablo, looking over the instructions.

Violet started spreading out the large sheet. "We'll definitely need to work together. Otherwise, it will get all twisted and tangled."

"These are probably the holes the hooks need to go through," said Deepak, holding up an edge.

Pablo and Violet each grabbed a side and stretched out the sheet. Violet pulled tightly, hooked her end up, and then went over to help Pablo. Deepak made sure

the sheet was straight and flat. With a few pulls and grunts, they finished the remaining sides.

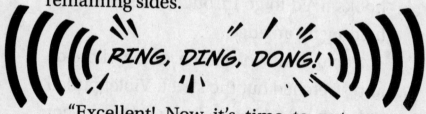

(((((((RING, DING, DONG!)))))))

"Excellent! Now it's time to put our model to the test." Dr. Crisp smiled as she

yelled into her watch, "Maker Maze, activate Maker Marbles!"

The floor began to rumble.

BOOM! SNAP! WHIZ! ZAP!

7

The light faded again. But this time there was a glow. It was the purple marbles! They were floating and slowly circling the room. The large black ball was floating, too! But Pablo, Violet, and Deepak could barely see it. The sheet was also glowing, but it was now green.

"That's so cool!" said Pablo. His face was tinted purple from the light of the marbles.

"What are those?" asked Deepak.

"I bet the black ball represents the black hole," said Violet.

"*Space*-tacular! You're correct," replied Dr. Crisp. She gave Violet a high five.

"Are the two purple marbles asteroids?" asked Pablo. Before Dr. Crisp could reply, he interrupted. "I mean, comets! Maybe they're comets?" Pablo said with a half-smile. He rubbed the back of his head. He didn't want to give any more wrong answers.

Dr. Crisp laughed. "Those marbles can be just about any space object you want." She clapped her hands twice. The floating purple marbles came to a sudden halt and zoomed toward her. She grabbed one in each hand.

With a gentle flick of her wrists, Dr. Crisp sent the glowing marbles sliding along the sheet. They rolled to a stop near the opposite edge.

"Unlike your friends and family back in the Newburg Meadow, space objects are always moving through dark energy. Even our planet Earth!" Dr. Crisp explained. She clapped her hands twice again and the balls flew back over to her. "And other objects that are nearby can affect the path they follow."

"Like a black hole?" asked Deepak.

"Exactly!" Dr. Crisp said. She clapped her hands four times.

The large black ball floated toward the center of the sheet. It lowered until it was sinking into the middle.

"Okay, Makers," began Dr. Crisp. "Now

it's time to put those magnificent minds to work! Try to figure out what black holes do to dark energy. That will help you figure out how they work."

Then Dr. Crisp raised both hands above her head and shouted, "Ready, set, THINK!"

Pablo, Violet, and Deepak examined the model space fabric.

Violet bit her lip. "I don't know about you two, but I can't tell what the black hole is doing to the dark energy."

Pablo had no idea, either. From what he could see, the model black hole was just sitting there. But he didn't want the others to know that.

"Well, black holes suck up everything that gets close to them," said Deepak, tugging his ear.

"Maybe black holes are like magnets!" Pablo suggested. "Maybe they attract space stuff that way?"

Deepak paused and thought. "I'm not sure. But we can test it out!"

"Yeah!" added Violet. "We can put the space balls on the sides of the sheet. If a real black hole works like a magnet, then they should be pulled over to the model black hole," Violet explained.

"Let's give it a try!" said Pablo.

But when they put one of the marbles on the edge of the sheet, nothing happened.

"Hmmmmm," said Deepak as he tugged his ear. "It didn't work."

Pablo felt his chest deflate again. He needed to think of another idea. And fast. "Maybe black holes are like a vacuum! And suck up space stuff!" he said.

"But that doesn't make sense," said Violet, shaking her head. "If black holes were like vacuums, then the marble would have still rolled toward it when we put it on the space fabric."

"Yeah, and we still don't even know what black holes are doing to the dark energy," added Deepak. He looked down at his Magnificent Maker Watch. It read forty-five minutes. "We need to hurry!"

This time, Pablo's shoulders sank along with his chest. He bowed his head.

"Pablo, what's wrong?" asked Violet. She put her hand on her best friend's arm.

Pablo was silent for several seconds. Then he lifted his head. His eyes were wet with tears. "I'm never going to be an astronaut, am I?"

8

Dr. Crisp clicked her heels and the light returned. She walked over to Pablo.

"Is everything okay here, Makers?" asked Dr. Crisp.

Pablo paused. And then sighed. He wiped away a tear and finally replied, "I don't think I'm smart enough to be an astronaut."

Dr. Crisp gasped and put her hand to her chest. "Pablo, why would you think something like that? Of course you're smart enough to be an astronaut! You're smart enough to become anything you want."

"But I can't even remember the difference between asteroids and comets," Pablo continued. He wiped away another tear. "I don't know how black holes work, either. And I probably won't know anything about whatever we'll learn in level three." He put his hands in his pockets and hung his head again.

"That's okay, Pablo." Dr. Crisp knelt to look him in the eye. "The Maker Maze is all about having fun and *learning*. Figuring stuff out!"

Pablo shook his head. "You don't understand, Dr. Crisp. Back in Puerto Rico, mis primos would tell me that I would only become an astronaut because my head was always in the clouds. My parents said to ignore them. But it's hard. And it makes me feel bad." Then he looked at Violet and Deepak. "When I kept messing up on the challenges, I felt like I was letting you down."

"But, Pablo," said Violet, "you're the smartest person I know!"

"Yeah," added Deepak. "You always have such good ideas. Remember, you figured out level three last time we all were here!"

"I'm so sorry your cousins would say those things to you," said Dr. Crisp. "It's not very nice. And it also is *not true*. You will become an astronaut, Pablo. Do you want to know how I know that?" Dr. Crisp asked.

Pablo nodded slowly.

"Because you *never* give up," said Dr. Crisp with a warm smile. "Not even when we only have thirty-five minutes left and still need to finish level two!"

Pablo smiled. Dr. Crisp was right. *I'm not a quitter,* he thought. "Thanks, Dr. Crisp. I promise to never, ever give up." Then he looked down at his watch. His eyes grew wide. "Wait, you weren't kidding! We only have thirty-five minutes left in *this* challenge!"

"Sorry to burst your bottle rocket, but yes!" replied Dr. Crisp. She clicked her heels and the lights turned off again.

"Uh-oh," said Deepak.

"It's okay," said Pablo. "We can get this done."

"I think we got a little ahead of ourselves before," said Violet.

Pablo agreed. "Yeah, I was trying to guess how black holes work before figuring out what they do to dark energy."

"Let's look at the sheet again," Deepak suggested.

The Makers inspected it carefully.

"How about we list everything we can observe and see if we get any ideas?" said Pablo.

Violet bent over and carefully studied the glowing sheet. "Whoa, I didn't pay attention to this before. But the model black hole must be pretty heavy. It's making the space fabric sag! A lot!"

"Excellent eyes!" said Dr. Crisp, raising her eyebrows up and down.

"Oh wow," said Deepak.

"So if this sheet represents dark

energy . . . ," Pablo thought out loud. He paused before finishing. "Maybe black holes *bend* dark energy?"

RING, DING, DONG!

"Loopy launchpads! Way to work together!" cheered Dr. Crisp.

"You did it!" said Violet and Deepak.

"*We* did it," replied Pablo. "And *we* still

need to figure out how black holes work," he said, tapping his watch.

"It must have something to do with bending dark energy," replied Deepak.

"That's it!" Pablo chased down the floating marbles and rolled them onto the sheet. This time, they didn't go straight to the other side.

BIZZAP!

"Whoa!" said Violet. "Where did they go?"

"They just disappeared!" exclaimed Deepak. "We can't even see them glow."

"It's gravity!" yelled Pablo with his fists in the air.

Violet and Deepak exchanged confused looks.

"I'm sensing that you're getting *pulled* toward the right answer!" cheered Dr. Crisp as she moonwalked across the floor.

"I can't believe I didn't think of this before!" said Pablo with his palm on his forehead. He began to explain his idea. "Things that have a lot of mass have a lot of gravity. Like Earth!"

"Mass? You mean things that weigh a lot?" asked Violet.

"No," replied Pablo. "Mass and weight are different. Something that is made up of a lot of *matter* has a lot of mass. But how much it *weighs* depends on how much gravity pulls on it."

"Yeah! We weigh less on the moon because it has less gravity," added Deepak. "But our *mass* is the same everywhere!"

"Even in Magnifica!" added Dr. Crisp with her finger in the air.

"Oooooooh! I think I get it," said Violet.

"I bet black holes have *a lot* of mass," Pablo continued. "That's why the big ball is the black hole and the smaller marbles are other space objects."

"So that means black holes must also have *really* strong gravity," Violet added.

"Yes!" Pablo turned to Dr. Crisp. "Can I get the marbles back?"

She smiled and clapped her hands twice.

BIZZAP!

The glowing purple marbles shot out of the model black hole and zoomed over to Pablo. He set one back on the edge of the sheet.

"Look underneath," Pablo said to Violet and Deepak.

"The marble bends dark energy, too!" said Deepak.

"But not nearly as much as the black hole," Violet pointed out.

"Exactly!" said Pablo. "A black hole

must bend dark energy so much that once a space object gets close enough, it can't escape! It just gets sucked in by all that gravity!"

RING, DING, DONG!

"Way to keep at it and *pull* through!" cheered Dr. Crisp with her fist in the air. "Magnificent Makers never give up!"

"Whew," said Violet, wiping her

forehead. "That was just about the hardest level ever."

"Well, I hope you all aren't too tired! We still have one level left and not much time!" replied Dr. Crisp. She retrieved the Maker Manual from her backpack. It snapped open and the pages began fluttering. They landed on a page that read:

LEVEL 3: NAME THAT PLANET

Go to secret door Q.

Dr. Crisp clicked her heels and light returned to the room. She aimed her watch at the ceiling. As she pressed a button on its side, a laser shot out! She scanned the ceiling until secret door *Q* opened.

"This way!" she shouted. Then she did a backflip and bounced off the sheet. She flew up through the door. "Hurry!" her voice echoed from above.

"I guess we should . . . follow her?" said Violet.

"Let's go," said Pablo. The Makers grabbed hands and jumped.

Secret door Q shut just as Pablo, Violet, and Deepak passed through it. They stumbled as their feet landed on the now closed door.

Pablo beamed. "I can't believe it!"

In the middle of the room, Dr. Crisp was standing in front of a row of small spaceships! A black M was painted on top of both wings, and two engines hung below them. Everyone was dressed in space suits again.

"Are we really going to fly these?" asked

Pablo, walking closer. His hands and feet jittered with excitement.

"You bet your jets!" replied Dr. Crisp.

"This is amazing," squealed Violet. "I'm going to drive a spaceship before I even drive a car!"

Deepak ran over to one of the ships and pressed his face against the windshield. "Whoa, there are a lot of buttons. And knobs." He pulled his face from the glass and asked Dr. Crisp, "Are they hard to fly?"

"Not at all! They pretty much fly themselves," she replied. "But we gotta hurry! We have to make it to three different planets, and we only have twenty-five minutes!"

"Three different planets?" the trio repeated.

"Yes!" Dr. Crisp began to explain the challenge. "For this final level, we are going to take these beauties for a spin." She gave one of the ships a pat. "With the help of our handy-dandy wormholes, we will hop around to three different planets. You'll have to guess which planet we are on based on what you know about their environments."

"But I don't even remember all the planets," said Violet. She bit her lip.

"I do!" said Pablo. He counted each name on a finger. "Mercury, Venus, Earth, Mars, Jupiter, Saturn, Uranus, and Neptune!"

"What about Pluto?" asked Deepak.

"Scientists used to call it a planet," explained Pablo. "But not anymore." He smiled.

Dr. Crisp gave Pablo a high five. Then she quickly ran over to a red button that was sticking out from the middle of one of the walls. She slammed it with her fist.

After a few moments of silence, the spaceships started to vibrate and hum. Then suddenly, their engines all turned on at once. The buttons on each dash-board lit up as the glass shields pulled back.

"Hop to it, Makers!" shouted Dr. Crisp as she jumped into her seat. Pablo, Violet, and Deepak climbed into their ships. The glass shields closed.

"Vroom, vroom!" cried Violet. "Let's go!"

Dr. Crisp pressed a black button on her dashboard and said, "Maker Maze,

activate wormhole!" The ceiling slid open, and the purple beam of light blasted down from above.

"Okay, Makers! Here we go!" said Dr. Crisp. "Hold down the green button on your right!"

The trio pressed their buttons at the same time.

SWIZZZZZZZZZ!

10

Pablo, Violet, Deepak, and Dr. Crisp shot through the wormhole. Their silver space-ships raced one after another until they took a sharp turn and popped out.

BIZZAP!

Their ships hovered above the dry and cracked ground. In the distance, volcanos shot bubbling lava into the air. Even from inside their spaceships, the Makers could tell it was hot.

Violet pressed the microphone button and said, "Is anyone else burning up?"

Little
beads of
sweat formed on
her forehead.

Deepak pulled on the neck of his shirt. "We must be close to the sun."

"There are two planets closer to the sun than Earth," said Pablo. He fanned his pink cheeks with his hands. "Mercury and Venus."

"Mercury is closest to the sun," said Deepak. "I bet that's where we are."

They waited for the Maker Maze jingle. But they only heard the bubbling of lava.

"Maybe I'm wrong," began Pablo. "But I remember learning that Venus was really hot, too. Something about its atmosphere."

Dr. Crisp pulled a folding fan out of a compartment in her spaceship. She snapped it open and said, "You're getting *warmer*!"

"I don't know if that's a good thing or a bad thing," said Violet.

Pablo and Deepak laughed.

"I remember learning that the air on Venus is so thick it traps heat," said Pablo. "Like a greenhouse! And I think that's what makes it the hottest planet in our solar system."

"Then we're definitely on Venus," added Violet.

RING, DING, DONG!

"Yes!" cheered the Makers.

"Hoppin' hot plates! Nice work!" said Dr. Crisp. "Now let's hightail it out of here before we melt!" Then she shouted, "Maker Maze, activate wormhole!"

They were suddenly surrounded by the beam of purple light.

SWIZZZZZZZZZ!

BIZZAP!

The spaceships were spit out of the wormhole. Within seconds, little ice crystals began to form on the front glass shield. Below them, the Makers could see thick, blue, slushy liquid swirling about.

"We must be way out in space," said Deepak. His teeth were chattering. "It's freezing!"

"Whoa! Look up there!" said Pablo, pointing toward the sky. "Moons!"

"I can see five of them!" said Violet.

"This must be Uranus!" shouted Pablo. "I forget how many moons it has. But it's a lot. And it's súper frío."

RING, DING, DONG!

"Rockin' rockets! Great job!" cheered Dr. Crisp.

"You're so good at this, Pablo!" said Deepak.

"For some reason I can remember all the special things about planets. But I can't remember the difference between an asteroid and a comet!" Pablo shook his head, smiled, and shrugged.

"Believe it or not," Dr. Crisp said, "Uranus has *twenty-seven* moons! I would give you a tour, but we need to hurry to our final planet!" Dr. Crisp opened the wormhole.

SWIZZZZZZZZZ!

BIZZAP!

The Makers arrived on a dusty, red planet. It was full of large rocks and craters. And it looked very familiar. . . .

But before anyone could guess where they were, Dr. Crisp's voice sounded throughout their spaceships.

"Makers, we have a problem!" she said. She held up her Magnificent Maker Watch. It was flashing purple!

"Only three Maker Minutes left!" said Violet.

"It's okay, I got this!" Pablo replied through is spaceship microphone. "We're on Mars! I knew it the minute we popped out of the wormhole!"

(((((RING, DING, DONG!)))))

"Way to save the day, Pablo!" cheered Dr. Crisp. Then she started pressing and swiping her watch. "I'm going to reprogram the wormhole to send us directly back to the main lab!"

In a flash of light, the wormhole appeared.

SWIZZZZZZZZ!

The Makers whizzed by comets,

asteroids, and maybe even a couple of planets. It was hard to tell. They were going so fast! Then suddenly, the spaceships disappeared. Pablo, Violet, and Deepak were tumbling closer and closer to the main lab!

BIZZAP!

"We made it!" said Deepak.

The Makers picked themselves up off the floor. They were right next to the long row of strange bugs in big glass jars. A few seconds later, Dr. Crisp came sliding out of the wormhole. But instead of landing next to the jars, she landed on top of them!

Crash!

Hundreds of creepy insects started flying and scurrying throughout the lab!

"You only have ten seconds!" Dr. Crisp yelled over the buzzing bugs. *"Hurry!"*

The trio swatted at the bugs as they

made their way through the swarm. They grabbed hands and leaped as high as they could.

BOOM! SNAP! WHIZ! ZAP!

Pablo, Violet, and Deepak tumbled through the binoculars and into the long grass of the Newburg Meadow just as everyone unfroze.

Violet shivered. "Ugh, I hope none of those bugs got in my hair." She shook out her curls.

"That was so gross," said Deepak.

"Mr. Eng's coming! Act normal," whispered Pablo.

"Did you all see that?" Mr. Eng asked, pointing to the sky. "Our first meteor of the night."

"Ummmm . . . ," Violet began.

"We missed it, Mr. Eng," Pablo interrupted. "We were helping Deepak find his binoculars."

Deepak forced a smile and shrugged.

"That's okay," said Mr. Eng. "There will be plenty more." Just then, two bugs started flying around his head. He swatted and swatted, but they wouldn't leave him alone! "Pesky mosquitos!"

"Those look like three-winged beetles!" said Violet.

"Three-winged beetles?" repeated Mr. Eng, still swatting. "That sounds a little—"

Pablo laughed and said, "Out of this world!"

Make your own creations!

⋛ MODEL A BLACK HOLE! ⋚

Always *make* carefully and with adult supervision!

MATERIALS

1 large ball (a soccer ball or basketball will work!)

1 small sheet or large pillowcase (or some other thin and smooth fabric)

2 small marbles

3 *magnificent* helpers

INSTRUCTIONS

1. Two helpers will pull the sheet or pillowcase tightly, one on each end. They should hold the fabric as still as possible. This fabric represents dark energy.

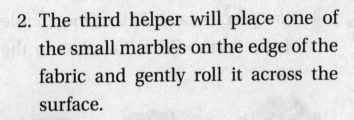

2. The third helper will place one of the small marbles on the edge of the fabric and gently roll it across the surface.

3. What happened? Record your observations.*

*You can create your own experiment sheet or ask your parent or guardian to download one at theannegriffith.com.

4. Now place a large ball in the middle of the fabric. What happens to the sheet?

5. Roll one of the small marbles across the fabric while the large ball is resting in the middle. What happens to the path of the marble? How is it different from the path it took without the large ball? Write down your results.

You can experiment with different-sized balls and marbles. How much mass does the ball need to have to change the path of the marble? You can also try rolling the marble at different speeds. How does this affect its path with and without the heavy ball? Get creative!

Your parent or guardian can share pictures and videos of your black hole on social media using #MagnificentMakers.

≶ MAKE YOUR OWN PLANET! ≶

MATERIALS

1 or more round balloons
1 cup of flour
2 cups of water
  bowl
  paint (acrylic works best, but
     other styles are fine, too!)
  spoon or whisk for stirring
  strips of scrap paper

INSTRUCTIONS

1. Mix one cup of flour and two cups of water in a bowl. Add more flour if the mix is too thin. Add more water if it is too thick. Set aside papier-mâché mix.

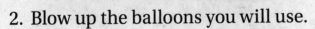

2. Blow up the balloons you will use.

3. Take the strips of scrap paper and dip them in the bowl of papier-mâché mix. Remove extra mix, and layer strips on the inflated balloon. For best results, add three layers, allowing layers to dry in between.

4. Allow all layers to dry. Drying time will depend on humidity. You can use a hair dryer to speed things up (but ask your parents first!).

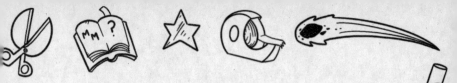

5. Once dried, you can paint your planet!*

*You can prime your planet with a layer of white paint, or paint directly on the dried scrap paper.

Get creative! What is the environment like on your planet? Is there life? Is it hot or cold? Write a short description of your planet to tell your audience more about it!

Your parent or guardian can share pictures and videos of your planet on social media using #MagnificentMakers.

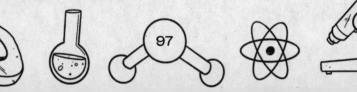

Missing the **Maker Maze** already?

Read on for a peek at the Magnificent Makers' next adventure!

Drip! Drop! Drip!

It was a rainy Monday morning at Newburg Elementary. Dark clouds filled the sky as rain splattered on the ground.

"I wish we could go outside today," said Violet. She rested her chin on her hands as she looked out the foggy window of Mr. Eng's third-grade classroom and sighed.

"I don't mind the rain," replied her best friend, Pablo. "It reminds me of Puerto Rico and summer storms. I loved playing in my abuela's backyard when it rained. She has this big mango tree. And I would catch the water drops that fell off its leaves in my mouth."

Violet smiled, then looked back out the window. "No mango trees in Newburg," she said. "Just mud and wet grass that I can't play in."

"Well, at least there aren't hurricanes in Newburg. Puerto Rico is beautiful, but sometimes storms turn into hurricanes," Pablo said. "It rains a lot, and the wind blows so fast and strong. Once, my tio's car got blown to the end of his street during a hurricane! He wasn't in it, though."

"Whoa, sounds scary!" Violet replied. "I wonder why Puerto Rico gets them and not Newburg."

"I'm not really sure." Pablo shrugged.

"But my abuela always says it's because the ocean is so warm."

"Hmmmm," Violet thought out loud. "Warm water and hurricanes . . ."

Mr. Eng interrupted her thinking. "Okay, class," he called from the front of the room. "As you can see, we won't be able to go outside today. But . . ." He raised his pencil in the air. "I do have a special surprise for you all."

The students' eyes grew wide. The room hummed with whispers of excitement.

"First, let's go over to the Science Space," Mr. Eng continued.

"Yes!" Violet and Pablo cheered. They stood up with the rest of the class and headed toward the back of the room.

Violet and Pablo were science-loving

best friends. One day, Violet was going to be a famous scientist and run her own lab. Pablo loved space and wanted to become an astronaut. But even when they weren't talking about science, Pablo and Violet were always together. They played soccer or double Dutch at recess. They also ate lunch with each other every day. And anytime they were in the Science Space, they worked in the same group.

Today, Violet and Pablo sat down at one of the round tables with the twins, Skylar and Devin. Skylar and Devin looked exactly alike. Except Skylar had puffball pigtails, and Devin had a buzz cut with a lightning bolt shaved into the side of his hair.

"I wonder what the surprise is!" Violet said as she sat down.

"I bet it's going to be cool," replied

Pablo. "We always do fun stuff in the Science Space."

Skylar nodded and smiled. But Devin just looked at his hands, which were folded in his lap.

Pablo tilted his head and asked, "Are you okay, Devin?"

Devin raised his eyes and offered a small shrug. "Yeah. I was just thinking."

"It's because—" began Skylar.

But Devin interrupted her. "It's okay. I'm fine."

"All right, class," Mr. Eng said. He stood next to a rectangular table. On top of it was a large object covered by a black sheet. "Are you ready for the surprise?"

"Yeah!" the students cheered.

Mr. Eng quickly pulled off the cover. A tall gray box with a clear front door sat on the table. The top part of the box had a fan that faced downward. At the bottom of the box sat a large blue bowl. Mr. Eng smiled proudly. But the room was full of confused faces.

Violet raised her hand. "Mr. Eng, um . . . what is that?"

Mr. Eng tapped the box and said, "This is a tornado machine! This week we are beginning a unit on weather and climate. And we are going to start off with a demonstration of how tornados form."

"That's so cool!" said Skylar.

"That box can make a tornado?" Violet asked.

"I can't wait to see this," added Pablo.

Acknowledgments

This journey wouldn't have been as easy or as fun without such wonderful support from my partner in life (and science), Jorge. Thank you, amor! I will be forever grateful, Mom and Dad, that you raised me in a home full of books. My love of reading started with you two. I love you, Dad, and I love and miss you immensely, Mom. Thank you to my own personal shooting star, Violeta. I love you to the end of the galaxy and back. Lila, my astronaut-in-training, you will definitely get to the moon one day. I can't wait to see you fly and shout "I love you!" from here on Earth. Thank you to the series illustrator, Reggie Brown, for bringing the Maker Maze world to life in such an amazing way. To the entire Random House team, Caroline Abbey, Tricia Lin, Lili Feinberg, and countless others, thank you! Team-work makes the dream work, and I am fortunate to have such an awesome team. Finally, I'd like to thank my wonderful agent, Chelsea Eberly. You're the best! Thank you for your continued guidance and support.